P9-DUI-538

DISCARD

THE OTHER CAST

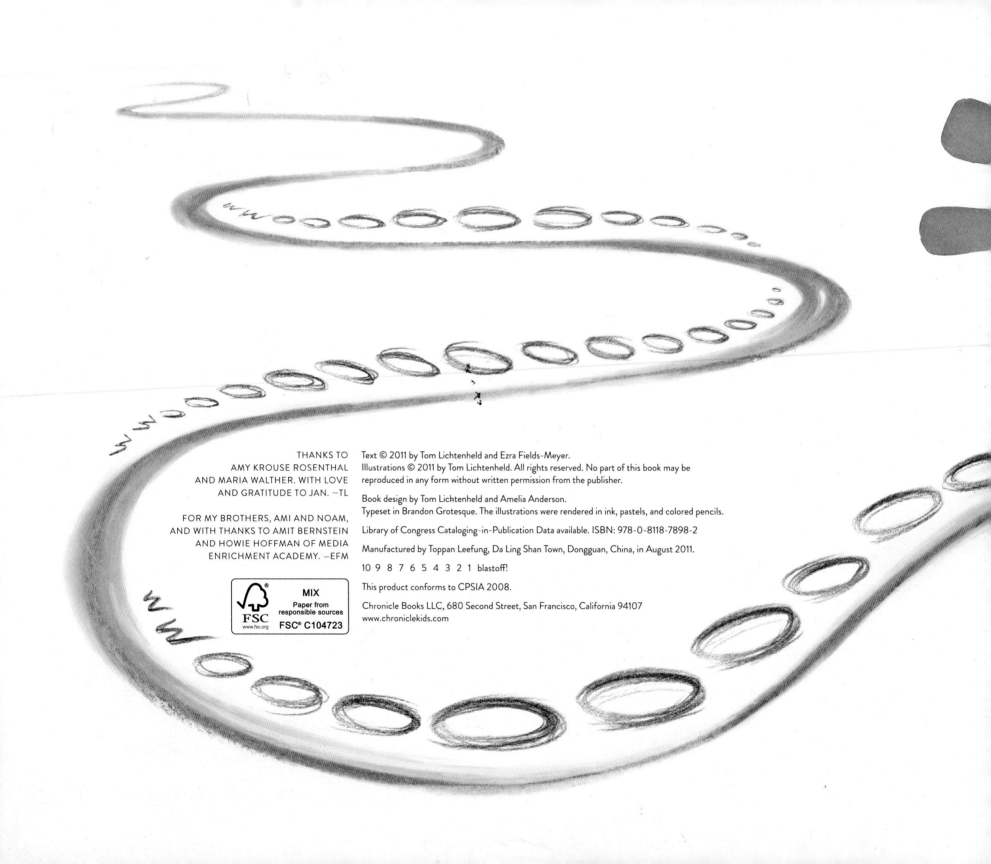

THANKS TO
AMY KROUSE ROSENTHAL
AND MARIA WALTHER. WITH LOVE
AND GRATITUDE TO JAN. —TL

FOR MY BROTHERS, AMI AND NOAM,
AND WITH THANKS TO AMIT BERNSTEIN
AND HOWIE HOFFMAN OF MEDIA
ENRICHMENT ACADEMY. —EFM

Text © 2011 by Tom Lichtenheld and Ezra Fields-Meyer.
Illustrations © 2011 by Tom Lichtenheld. All rights reserved. No part of this book may be
reproduced in any form without written permission from the publisher.

Book design by Tom Lichtenheld and Amelia Anderson.
Typeset in Brandon Grotesque. The illustrations were rendered in ink, pastels, and colored pencils.

Library of Congress Cataloging-in-Publication Data available. ISBN: 978-0-8118-7898-2

Manufactured by Toppan Leefung, Da Ling Shan Town, Dongguan, China, in August 2011.

10 9 8 7 6 5 4 3 2 1 blastoff!

This product conforms to CPSIA 2008.

Chronicle Books LLC, 680 Second Street, San Francisco, California 94107
www.chroniclekids.com

FSC
www.fsc.org
MIX
Paper from
responsible sources
FSC® C104723

E.MERGENCY!

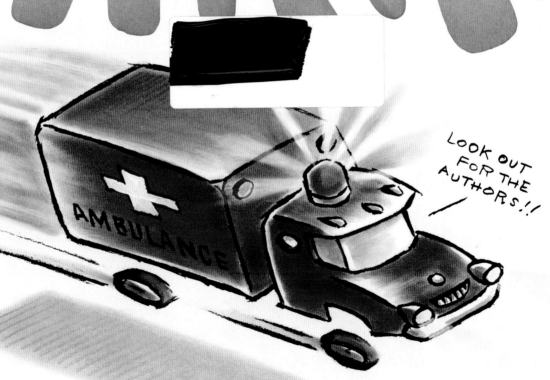

LOOK OUT FOR THE AUTHORS!!

AMBULANCE

chronicle books · san francisco

TOM LICHTENHELD

EZRA FIELDS-MEYER

ALL THE LETTERS LIVED
TOGETHER IN A BIG HOUSE.

HEY LOOK —
ALPHABET SOUP!

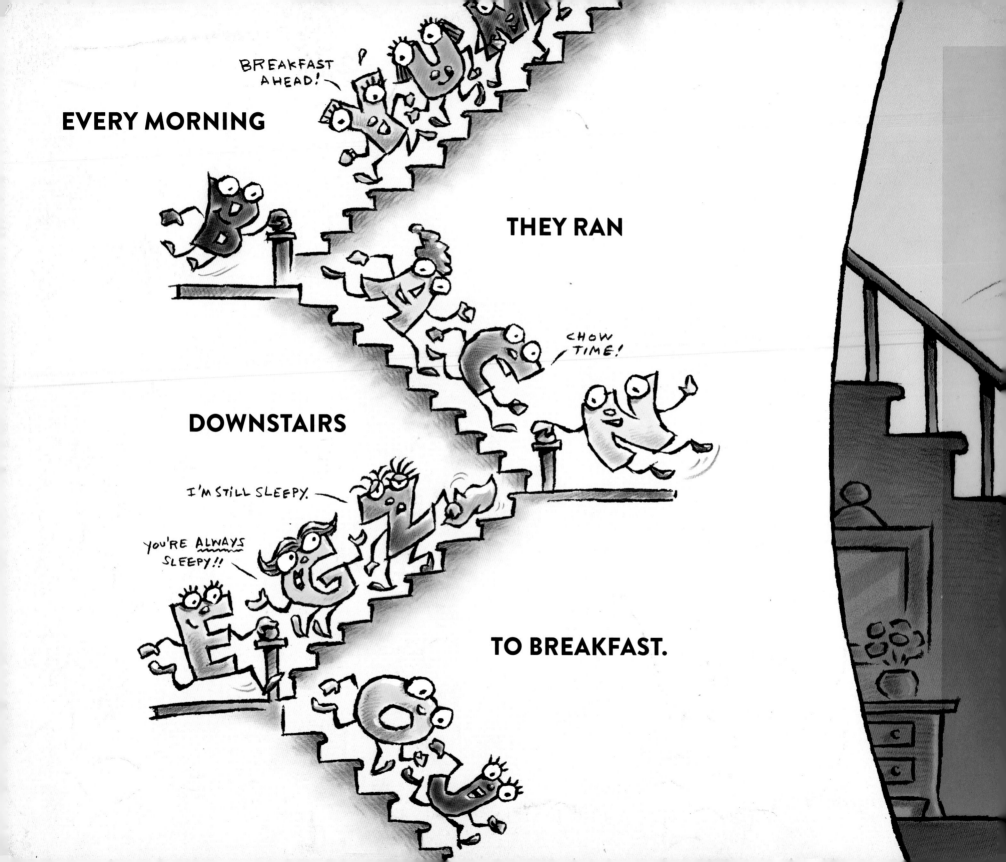

ONE MORNING, **E** CAME DOWN THE
STAIRS A LITTLE TOO FAST.

EVERYONE CAME RUNNING

TO SEE WHAT HAPPENED.

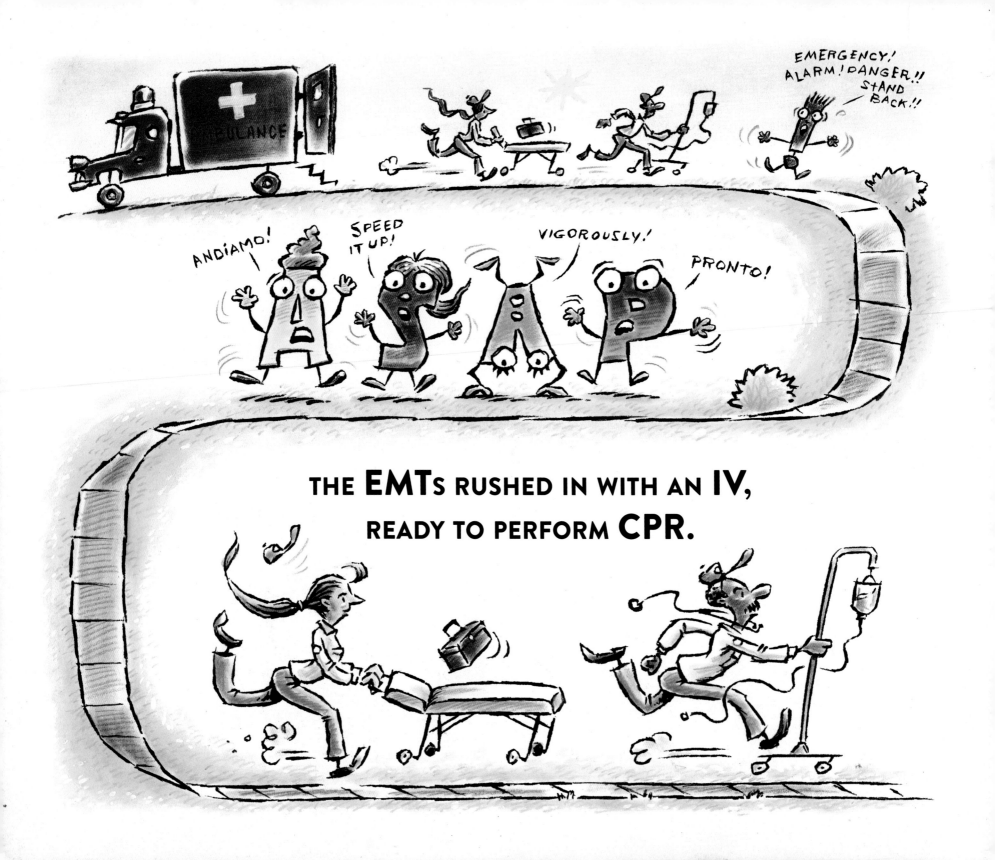

THE **EMT**s RUSHED IN WITH AN **IV**,
READY TO PERFORM **CPR.**

AND THE REST OF THE LETTERS TALKED IT UP ON THE TALK SHOWS.

O DID HIS BEST FILLING IN FOR **E**,
BUT THE RESULTS WERE QUITE CONFUSING.

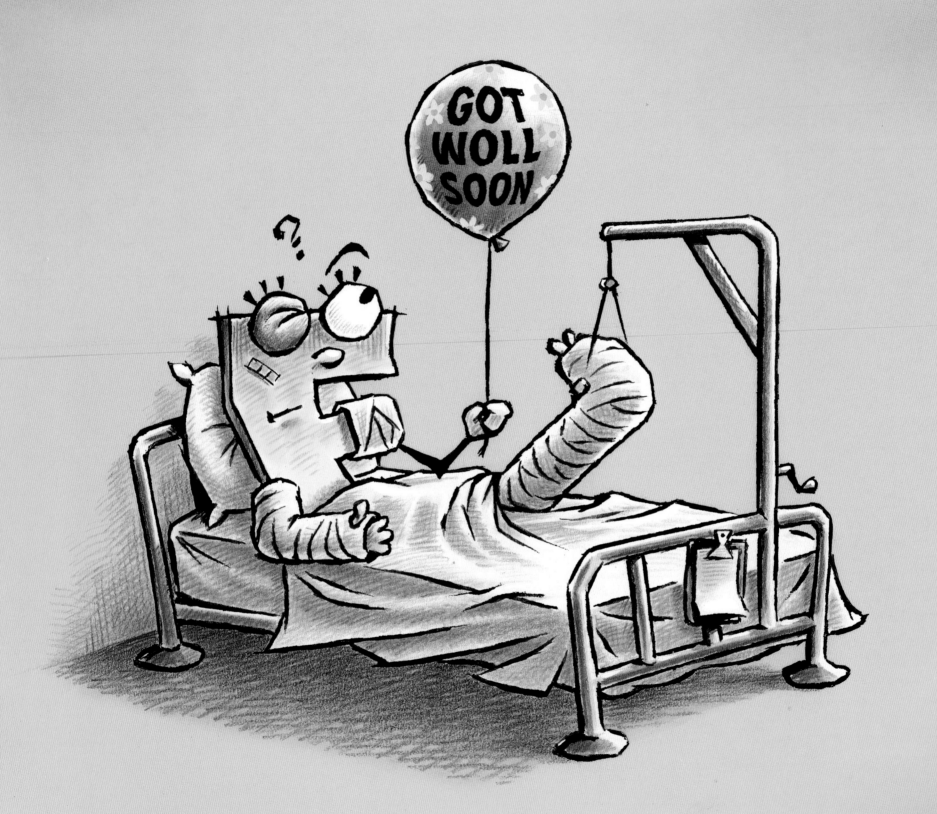

TO MAKE MATTERS WORSE, **E** WASN'T GETTING BETTER.
THE **MDs** COULDN'T FIGURE OUT WHY.

A DECIDED THEY NEEDED TO TAKE A TRIP TO SPREAD THE WORD ABOUT THE LETTER.

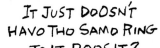

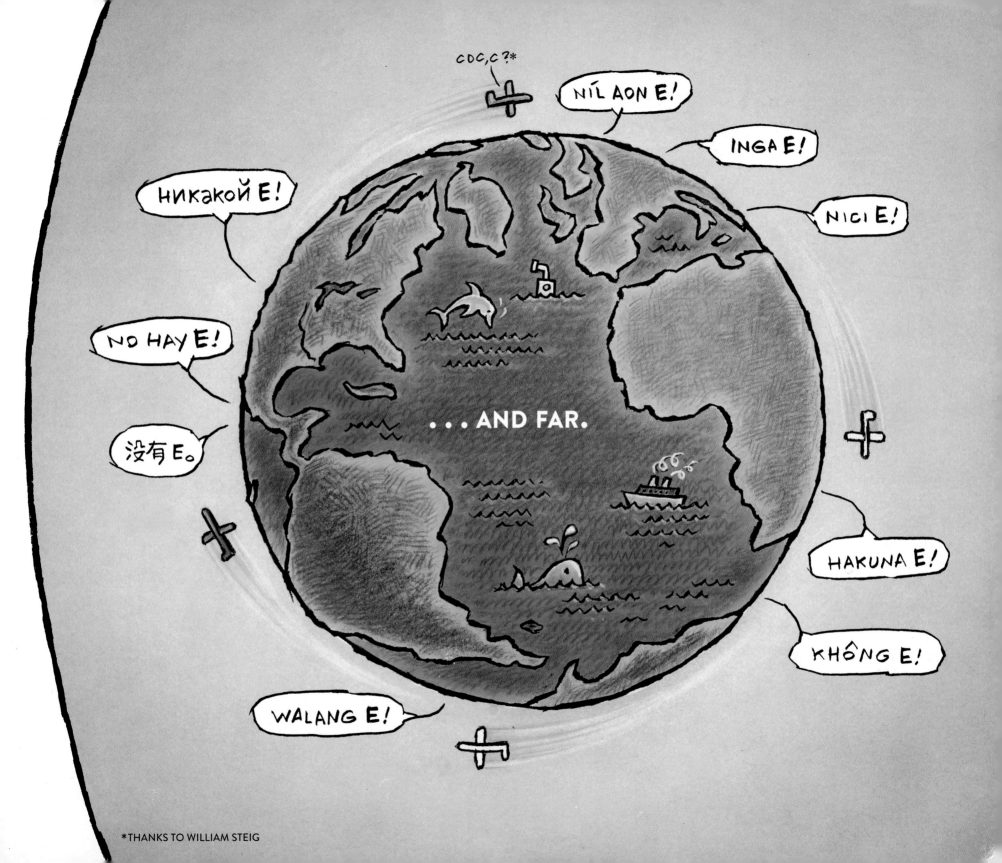

*THANKS TO WILLIAM STEIG

WHEN THEY GOT HOME, E STILL WASN'T RECOVERED.

THE LETTERS HAD A PROBLEM.

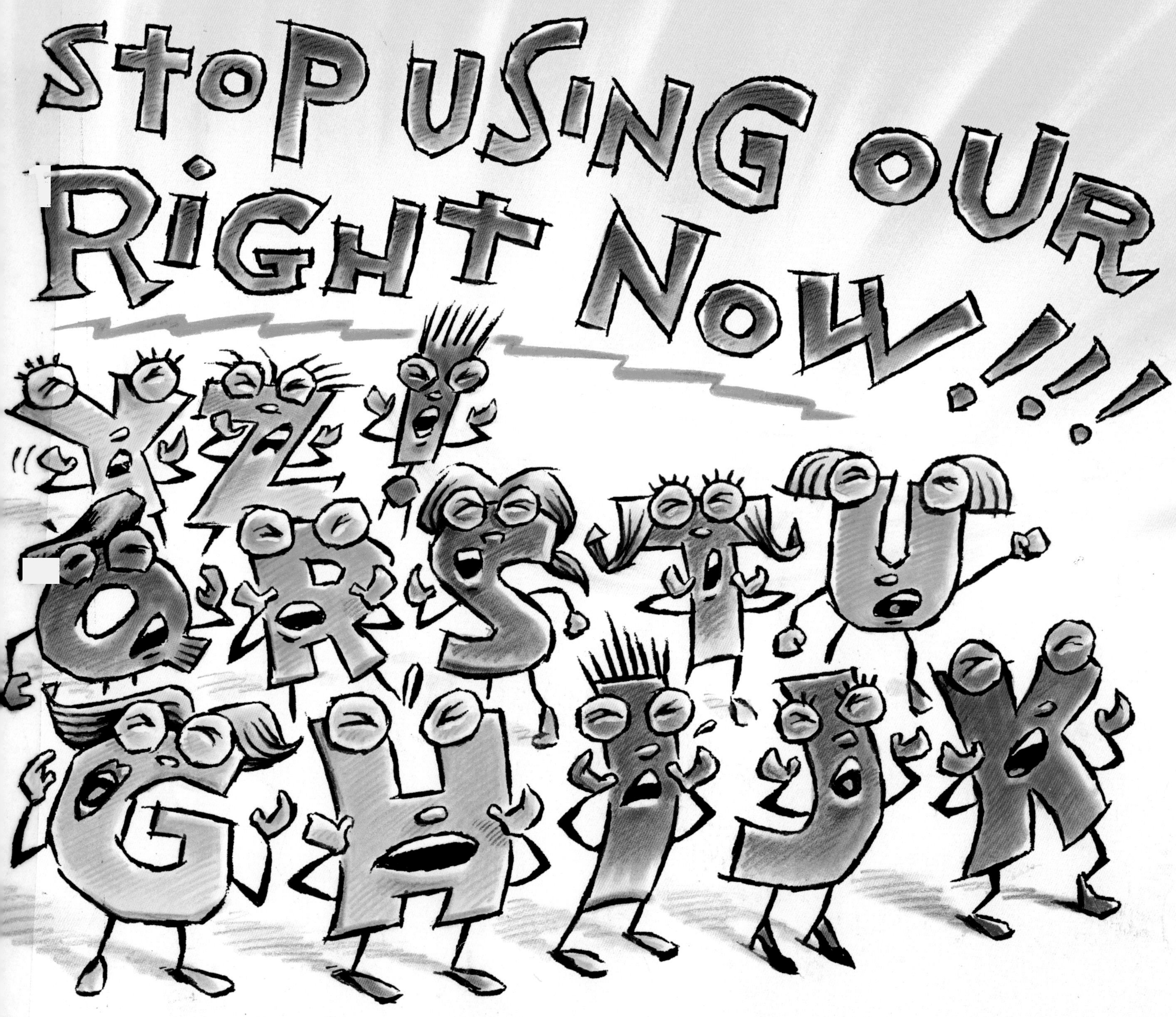
STOP USING OUR
RIGHT NOW!!!

SO THO LAST PORSON
USING YOU-KNOW-WHO
STOPPOD.

THAT'S BOTTOR.

← CAST-
OFF

QUICK AS A WINK, SHO
WAS OUT OF BOD AND ROADY
TO GO BACK TO WORK.

JUST IN TIMO FOR . . .

th**E E**nd.